llama llama meets the babysitter

by **Anna Dewdney** and **Reed Duncan**
illustrated by **JT Morrow**

VIKING

Llama Llama having toast.
Llama loves this meal the most—
the start of every happy day!

Mama has some things to say.

I have something new to talk about.
Tonight I will be going out.
Gram can't come as normal, but
I have a plan you'll like a lot.

Just as always, we'll have dinner,
and then you'll have a **BABYSITTER!**

Someone to be here
while I'm gone.
Don't worry, dear,
it won't be long.

A baby-*what* . . . ? That's not the same.
Does this sitter have a name?

You've met Molly. She's fun and kind.
Once she gets here, you won't mind.

We're not the same, yes, that's true,
but she will take good care of you.

Will she want to ride my bike?
Will she read the books I like?
Will she play my favorite games?
Will she even know my **name** . . . ?

Of course she knows you,
Llama dear.
You'll have fun
while I'm not here.

Will she know to make my snack?
And what if you do not come back?!

Llama Llama, you'll be fine.
Molly does this all the time.
No need to fret. No need to moan.
Of course I will be coming home!

Llama Llama feeling sad.
Llama getting oh so **MAD**.

Llama's brain starts to fizz . . .
Who does this sitter think she is?!

I won't be nice. I won't have fun.
Instead I will **run,**

The doorbell rings—now she's here!
Come say hello, Llama dear!

Llama peeks around the door.
Wait . . . here's someone
he's seen before!

I know *you*—you scoop ice cream!

Yes, I'm Molly.

Llama beams.

What's in the bag?

I've brought samples!
Vanilla, chocolate,
and pineapple!

Mama Llama blows a **kiss**.
I think you both are fine with this.

Mama's gone now,
out the door.

Treats with Molly—and so much more!

Play in the yard, jump up and down,
kick the ball and run around.

Ice cream, reading, hide-'n'-seek.
Llama could do this all week!

Time to brush
and off to bed.

Fluff the pillow
for Llama's head.

Molly and Mama are not the same,
but Llama's glad this sitter came.

Almost asleep, and not alone:
Molly's here—Mama's almost **home**.

Light from the door—just a crack . . .

Mama Llama, you came back!

Can Molly come again next week?

For all the babysitters who had to deal with us . . .

—A.D. and R.D.

To Deborah Wolfe and Lisa Pomerantz.
Thanks for everything. —J.T.M.

VIKING
An imprint of Penguin Random House LLC New York

First published in the United States of America by Viking,
an imprint of Penguin Random House LLC, 2021

Copyright © 2021 by the Anna E. Dewdney Literary Trust

Penguin supports copyright. Copyright fuels creativity, encourages diverse voices, promotes
free speech, and creates a vibrant culture. Thank you for buying an authorized edition
of this book and for complying with copyright laws by not reproducing, scanning, or
distributing any part of it in any form without permission. You are supporting writers and
allowing Penguin to continue to publish books for every reader.

Viking & colophon are registered trademarks of Penguin Random House LLC.

Visit us online at penguinrandomhouse.com.

LIBRARY OF CONGRESS CATALOGING-IN-PUBLICATION DATA IS AVAILABLE
ISBN 9780593350331

Manufactured in China

1   3   5   7   9   10   8   6   4   2

Text set in ITC Quorum Std

Closely following the style of Anna Dewdney, the art for this book was created
with oil paint, colored pencil, and oil pastel on primed canvas.

The publisher does not have any control over and does not assume any responsibility for
author or third-party websites or their content.